Stone Soup

Writing and art by kids, for kids

Editor's Note

We don't often talk about politics in the print magazine of *Stone Soup*. This is in large part because we work so far ahead on each issue that any attempt to speak to current events will inevitably be outdated by the time the magazine arrives at your door. Instead, we publish more timely and topical submissions—about the pandemic, the election, Black Lives Matter, and more—on our blog.

However, in this issue, you will read Cora Burch's poems about her experience of the pandemic as well as one about President Trump, a poem she wrote before the storming of the capitol that now feels eerily prescient.

You will also encounter Steven Cavros's "The Sewer People," a story about an imaginary society and government that forces us to think about our own—much like George Orwell's novel *Animal Farm*.

I encourage you to try writing a poem or story that is about politics without being about our current politics.

Finally, in these pages, you will find the final installment of Ariana Kralicek's novella, *The Trials and Tribulations of Swifty Appledoe*. I hope reading about Swifty has put a smile on your face and maybe even inspired you try something new!

On the cover:
Parachuting in City Lights
(Watercolor)
Sloka Ganne, 10
Overland Park, KS

Ed̶

̶r

& Special Projects
Sarah Ainsworth

Design
Joe Ewart

Stone Soup (ISSN 0094 579X) is published eleven times per year—monthly, with a combined July/August summer issue. Copyright © 2021 by the Children's Art Foundation–Stone Soup Inc., a 501(c)(3) nonprofit organization located in Santa Cruz, California. All rights reserved.

Thirty-five percent of our subscription price is tax-deductible. Make a donation at Stonesoup.com/donate, and support us by choosing Children's Art Foundation as your Amazon Smile charity.

POSTMASTER: Send address changes to Stone Soup, 126 Otis Street, Santa Cruz, CA 95060. Periodicals postage paid at Santa Cruz, California, and additional offices.

Stone Soup is available in different formats to persons who have trouble seeing or reading the print or online editions. To request the braille edition from the National Library of Congress, call +1 800-424-8567. To request access to the audio edition via the National Federation of the Blind's NFB-NEWSLINE®, call +1 866-504-7300, or visit Nfbnewsline.org.

Submit your stories, poems, art, and letters to the editor via Stonesoup.submittable.com/submit. Subscribe to the print and digital editions at Stonesoup.com. Email questions about your subscription to Subscriptions@stonesoup.com. All other queries via email to Stonesoup@stonesoup.com.

Check us out on social media:

StoneSoup
Contents

Wild City (Watercolor and Sharpie)
Saylor Creswell, 8
New York, NY

The Road Home

For the first time ever, the author is given permission to go outside alone—in New York City

By Shriyans Boddu, 11
New York, NY

I stared longingly out my bedroom window on the thirty-third floor of my New York City apartment building. I could almost hear the babbling of New Yorkers walking down the labyrinth of streets that unfolded in front of me. My skin tingled in the warmth of the bright summer sun radiating down on the Earth. My mouth salivated as I imagined the countless delicacies in all of the magnificent restaurants, which were scattered across the streets.

However, when I opened my eyes, I saw the distance between me and the life I desired. I felt as if I were a spectator in an exciting ball game, wanting to play. I envied them all for the one gift they had that I didn't possess, a gift I had craved for so long: the gift of pure and complete freedom.

Suddenly, I heard the click of the key unlocking the door. I detached my gaze from the window and wandered to the door as my mom walked in. She had a casual posture, with her black handbag slung across one shoulder. Her gentle embrace brought me warmth and security.

"You were bored today, weren't you?" my mom asked. I simply sighed in return. Camp would not start for an entire week, and my anticipation of its fun and joy was dwarfed by the monotonous passing of time, during which I did chiefly nothing. Taking pity on me, my mom uttered the sentence that would change my life in the days to come: "I'll speak with Dad and see if there is anything you can do."

Knowing not to get my hopes up, I just shrugged my shoulders. And upon noticing my mother's tired face, I put on a big smile and said in an enthusiastic voice, "Okay. Thanks." The rest of the evening passed uneventfully.

The next morning, my eyes were suddenly flooded with light as I rolled over on my bed and reluctantly got up. I then stared out my window and saw crisp blue skies, mere wisps of clouds, and the bright summer sun.

"Hey, Shri!" my mom called.

"Yeah?" I replied, nearly jumping off my bunk bed in response to my mother's voice.

"Always keep your phone with you, and don't cross the streets when there is a red light," she said. After this command, my mom went on and on about safety, but I was perplexed.

"Don't cross the street when there's a red light?" I repeated, my neurons firing a mile a millisecond trying to explain this phenomenon. "But I'll be inside the entire day," I stated flatly.

My mom started to laugh, and it was then that I knew something was amiss. "Don't make me regret this," she muttered as she sucked in a deep breath and once again started talking. "I'm granting you permission to walk outside alone," she stated.

I was downright shocked. I had been asking for this privilege for years, and I had always been turned down. I had eventually given up. "But why?" I asked, and immediately wished I hadn't. I prayed that she wouldn't take back this privilege.

"You're almost a fifth-grader. Your dad and I think you should have this experience," she said. With that, she ran to the door and I was left alone to contemplate my mother's statement. I live on the Upper East Side, a friendly community in general, but one that has its share of dangers and obstacles. My gaze naturally drifted toward the window, and it was then, at that moment, the choice became clear: I could finally have the life I had coveted for so long.

Suddenly, my phone started to buzz, long and loud. I put my hands over my ears, praying it would stop. I had received nearly eighty messages, each one of them from my mom regarding safety. I glanced around my apartment, and then I looked at the door.

Taking a deep breath, I grabbed my phone and tentatively stepped outside my apartment into the neat hallway with high ceilings and chandeliers and an elaborate jade-green carpet. I did not know what I had expected from this mere action. I anticipated a feeling of freedom, but my feelings seemed to be entirely quotidian and regular. Despite my best attempts to have hope, it seemed to fade away. *I'll feel something when I walk outside*, I thought.

Nevertheless, as I got into the elevator and pressed "Lobby," causing the elevator to start descending, my feelings of doubt returned.

The elevator reached the lobby with a ding, and I apprehensively crept toward the automated doors. The doors, which, when opened, would lead to freedom.

When I'd finally stepped outside of the apartment building, the warmth of the beaming sun spread throughout my body, from synapse to axon, and a sense of joy overcame me. As I wandered around, I saw the neat and elegant streets of NYC with all of the diversified shops, hotels, apartment buildings, and even the occasional hospital magically crammed into one mere city block. It was as if I were wearing glasses; I was seeing the same picture, magnified. I saw little babies attempt to master the motor skills required to stand up, and the resulting smiles of the passersby. After that, I went into a huge park where I started to play for a little while.

After many more minutes of in-depth "tourism," I felt the stress of my studies and the responsibilities of becoming a fifth-grader disappear and dissolve into thin air. I felt my shoulders sigh a breath of relief and gratitude as the burdens of everyday life somehow sprouted wings and started to fly. My mind no longer concentrated on my worries and problems but rather on the countless attractions around me.

I was admiring the flowers in full bloom and was engrossed in their pure beauty when the laughter of a boy finally brought my attention back to the real world.

I glanced at my watch. *Was it 3:45 already?* I started to feel my legs ache. *Had I really been playing for that long?* I vaguely recalled a text from my mom informing me to be home at 4:00. I suddenly realized the truth in the old adage "Time flies when you are having fun."

As I started to head home, I came to a sudden halt. I felt my entire body tense up as I scanned my surroundings. I looked in all directions, and I saw nothing with even an ounce of familiarity in my line of sight. Sweat started to trickle down my forehead, and my eyes started to well up with tears. I quickly realized that the intimidating structures, which towered far above me, bore no resemblance to the ones near home. In a fit of frustration, I stomped with so much force my knees buckled, and my balance ceased to exist. "Need some help?" a voice asked. I tilted my head and to my surprise saw a boy, no older than me, twirling a basketball in his hand.

"No," I said, trying to stand up and collect myself.

"Really," he said, his lips curving upward. I looked at the boy: his eyes were the lightest shade of blue, and his pale face was mostly covered by his blond hair. He was sporting a Knicks outfit from his T-shirt to his shoes.

With what I hoped was a nonchalant tone, I asked, "Do you know where 'here' is?"

"Eighty-sixth and Second," he said. "Are you lost?"

"Of course not," I lied. There was no way I would get home in time. Suddenly, an idea started to take shape in my head. "Do you know where the Q train is?" I asked hopefully.

"Look behind you," he said. I felt my face turn red yet again, and I despised my lack of observation and momentary blindness.

"Thanks again," I yelled as I took off and rounded the corner. Waving one more time, I practically sprinted toward the escalator. It was already 3:54.

With a nod of gratitude for my mom's million messages, which had included advice to bring a MetroCard, I swiped my MetroCard into the metal turnstile and ran as fast as my legs could carry me. Without a second thought, I leaped into the train just in time. As the voice said, "Doors closing," I took a seat and for the umpteenth time, glanced at my watch. It read 4:02. The train rumbled and took off while I glanced out the window and saw the color black.

Minutes later, the train came to a screeching halt, "This is 96th street."

I put my face in my hands as I got off the train. *Why? Why was this happening to me?* I then kicked the large grey pole as hard as I could. A sudden pain started to sink in, but my rage easily dwarfed it.

To relax, I decided to use some of my mother's teachings on deep breathing. I was able to calm my racing and raging thoughts, which then allowed me to think rationally. I took a deep breath as my mother had taught me, making my mind clear at first and then focusing on my problem.

Then it hit me. If I came here by one train, then the opposite train would be my savior. In seconds, I cheerfully hopped aboard the downtown train to head home.

A Tangled World (iPhone 8)
Elodie Weinzierl, 11
Waban, MA

Three Poems

By Rainer Pasca, 14
Bay Shore, NY

Rainer's Mind

I was in a forest with nothing
but my mind. It opened
a little bit—

lifted its mouth like a shark.
Suddenly, a bird.
Snap, said my mind.
Delicious! I didn't
even say hello.
I just walked home.

Rumi on the Table

I'm thinking of nothing.
My head is empty like a garbage can.
Oh, I can't write this poem.
Hey, look. Rumi is on the table.
Rumi, why don't we make a poem?
He's purring!
Awww, he is purring the poem.
I love you, Rumi.
You're the king of gold.

Hurricane

Irene was a nasty dream. Waking
up with colors
in my eyes, watching her
falling down inside
my mouth. I was
covering my ears flat
as possible. The rusty wagon dripping old
and wet, it slowed—
stopped.

My hurricane is me—
I could not know. My flashlight told
me that. Fueling myself to
push back into normal,
I could convince myself
that was
just
a nasty dream

Leading Bridge (Nikon D5100)
Claire Lu, 13
Portola Valley, CA

Four Poems

By Cora Burch, 13
Van Nuys, CA

Calm

It is 4:00 AM.
Not quite,
more like 4:02,
or 4:05.
But it doesn't
matter really,
like how the virus
will one day leave
and we will still
wash our hands
every time we
get home from
the store.
I am sitting in bed
reading a book I
love, a story that
leaves me at peace
every time I read it.
It's calming,
in a strange way,
even though there
is a conflict,
like how the sky
can still be that

beautiful electric
indigo of 4:00 AM,
or 4:02,
and in the back
of my mind
I know that
people are still dying.

Right

When my best friend walks
a foot too close I flinch.
That doesn't feel right.
Is it possible to
walk upon the earth
hand in hand,
to rise up and touch stars
that are just reachable,
without touching once?
It feels impossible.

Bike Shopping

I am on my dad's computer
scanning Craigslist and
stressing over the
purchase of a new bike,
as I am adamant
about getting one that
doesn't have a sloped bar,
which is a trait of stereotypically
"girl" bikes,
and I don't want one with
a horizontal bar either,
a "men's" bike,
so the one I would
really like would have a
half bar,
like my current bike,
that sits without curve on a
diagonal,
and look—
here is a red one,
with the bar that I want,
simple gear shifters,
and just my size of 16,
and it is listed as
a women's bike,
but I will get it anyway,
so my dad and I
schedule a trip
to pick it up,
and it takes less time than
formerly thought,
only thirty minutes with the
pandemic and all and—
oh right.
The pandemic.

Cornered

Deep in the White House,
maybe in a closet,
the door is shut and
barricaded from
the inside by an
armoire and a heavy sofa.
To his left you might see a
machine gun.
To his right is a decoy:
a rifle labeled
the 2nd Amendment.
The man's face is in shadow.
On the wall, his country's
upside-down flag hangs crookedly.
On the wall opposite,
the flag of treason has been
nailed to the wall
beside the hanging skeletal figure of a
young man.
A Bible sits,
brand new and yet covered in dust,
on a barren shelf behind him.
On the back wall,
a flat-screen TV
frames his face.
There is a whiteboard
deep inside the closet.
An Expo marker is tied on a string
to the corner of the board.
It has been recently erased.
A picture of his daughter has been
tacked to the board with a
round black magnet,
her face false with make-up.
If you look closely,

you will see that
his right shoelace is undone.
The hem of his pants are crooked.
Perched on the bridge of his nose
is a pair of borrowed glasses.
If he knew these things,
if he could see these things,
he would not let them slide.
The man is cornered.
He has cornered himself.

Untitled (Acrylic)
Halil, age unknown
Syria

Artist description of the piece (translated from Arabic):

There is something hiding behind the painting. There is a ghost behind it. It is the ghost of someone. (Who?) (No answer to that.) It is not me (says the artist); it is another girl who is afraid. The ghost frightens people, but it does not hurt them. (What does the girl in the picture say?) The girl (in the picture) says the ghost came to her. (What does the girl say to you about the ghost?) She told me so we can help her.

Ghost of a Killer (Acrylic)
Suzan, 10
Syria (Kurdish)

Artist description of the piece (translated from Arabic):

The colors are nice. Behind the picture, there is a ghost. It is the ghost of a killer.

Both paintings were created with the support of the "Inside-Outside Project".

About the Project

Millions of children who have escaped from war, persecution, and climate change are now living in refugee camps, or in host countries far from their homes. The work that appears here is a part of *Stone Soup*'s growing collection of creative expression by young people whose lives have been upended by such conflict throughout the world.

The Sewer People

The trouble begins when the sewer people decide to form a government

By Steven Cavros, 9
Hollywood, FL

Now once, long ago, on June 12, 2027, a stray banana peel found its way into the sewers of Orlando, Florida. It travelled through the sewers for twenty minutes, and then it at last came to the very bottom of the sewers, to a deep puddle. Like all the junk there, it joined itself to a sea of junk, and nine minutes later, a little human-like creature with frail limbs stood where eighteen or so bits of junk had come together.

All the sewer people came from junk, of course. Hundreds, thousands of the sewer people there were— made from all the junk in the sewers— and no junk ever left the sewers as a banana peel or bit of ripped paper.

The sewer people had no government, no economy, no friends. All ignored them, didn't care for a moment that they existed, ignored them terribly, TERRIBLY. They were forgotten and lost.

All the troubles of the world began when an important sewer person, Dirt, proposed a government to his small ring of friends, Junk and Meaningless. But they could not create a government without the support of the 18,000 little frail-limbed sewer people they shared the sewers with. They called a meeting, but in vain, as it ended in chaos. Another meeting, then another, was held until many sewer people approved a government. But as that meeting closed, a new problem arose: how would they make a government, and who would be on it?

The idea was simple enough: they needed a leader who would have a title and make decisions, and no one but him would have power. Of course, it can be seen the sewer people were terribly mistaken about the nature of government and laws. For the laws said, "Do no wrong"—of course leaving much to be desired, as the law of "Do no wrong" was twisted by different perceptions of wrong.

Now one day, Dirt was speaking with Junk and Meaningless. Anyone just joining to listen would have been very lost, so you will be briefed: they were arguing over the meaning of right and wrong. Dirt was screaming, yelling, proving his point badly, with useless, wasted words. Dirt's fist struck Meaningless as Junk raised his arms in surrender, panting, agreeing hastily that killing was wrong, a subject that had been key to the argument. They were so new to governments and hierarchies and laws, they were still debating over whether murder was wrong when Dirt was elected chief of the sewer people.

The poor sewer people fled their failing government, some in terror, mostly drowning in puddles or being filleted in sewer grates. Still, some remained, fighting for a strong government. Dirt stayed to fight for the government he had always hoped to achieve. But then one night he was forced by armed mobs of sewer people to surrender his place as leader. Strange things occurred while Dirt lay in chains on a hard, cold floor—like Junk's refusal to be elected to the chief board of the sewer people.

Junk was sitting comfortably in an old soda can, his home—and a very luxurious one at that. He suddenly beheld, through a window hole cut in the side of his can home, a little sewer man running up to his wide-open door.

The little sewer man entered and hastily regurgitated some words written down on a piece of parchment—to us a shred, to them a scroll. The words Junk made out were something like this, to his ears: "Thee, thou art, appointment, chief?" Well, "chief" he could make out, but it surprised the messenger greatly when he was shooed away, after being dubbed an "irking parasite" by the would-be most important sewer person. Junk left, and was presumed dead, but his body was never found submerged in a sewer puddle, and his flesh and hair were never found in sewer grates. Junk's refusal to

be chief of the sewer people made Meaningless the chief sewer person.

Meaningless believed in a strong government but still wanted to make fair government, with equal division of power. His government began nine days after he took office, leaving him with only a small amount of power on a seventy-person cabinet. Meaningless began to call his government design weak, yet he was still very respected. Eventually, he became strong again, and many of those on the cabinet were cruelly executed. Now one day, Meaningless fled the sewers, being strongly disliked, and no government was kept among the sewer people.

One night, many years after Meaningless had fled the sewers, Junk's son was growing old, and the moon came out over the sewers, and he said: "Tonight, all, is our night—to live life, to crawl from these sewers, even if we never see a night like this again."

And so, all of the sewer people climbed from the sewers, those delegates of the underbelly of society, and danced and talked and ate scraps they found until the sun rose and shone down on them, and they all quickly clambered back to the sewers, sewers where they had been before.

But none ever forgot that day: even when the day came when the sewers fell apart, broke, were excavated, the memory still hung in the air somewhere else. In another place. In the poor old sewers, even as the pipes were carted away and the street crew came, garbage men and construction workers, all never knowing what had once been there. Once, long ago.

Happiness Comes to America

For the author, a bad hair day turns into a bad hair week

By Happiness Neema, 11
Kigoma, Tanzania; Chicago, IL

All names in this story have been changed for privacy.

A few years ago, my mom and dad, my two older brothers, and I moved from a refugee camp in Tanzania to Chicago. Now I'm eleven years old. My name is Happiness.

One Sunday night I sat down on my usual pillow on the couch between Mama's legs so she could fix my hair. She divided it into skinny braids and then pulled them into an elastic band on top of my head.

"Okay, I'm done," she said. (Sometimes she talks to me in English instead of Kirundi.)

I ran to the bathroom and checked in the mirror. I felt sad. Mama has time to do my hair just once a week, so I would look like this till next Saturday or Sunday.

I didn't say anything to Mama. I just put on my pajamas and went to bed, hoping that everything would be okay in the morning.

The next day I went to school with all the braids sticking up. I wanted to sit by my friends Daniella and Ruby, but my teacher asked me to sit between Rosa and Miguel instead. While we waited for class to start, we played a game. But then Miguel began making little jokes about my hair.

"Your hair looks like an onion," he said. "Some kind of vegetable ... No, it looks like a tomato!"

I wanted to cry. But I just stayed quiet. All day I thought about it.

During the passing period, I told Ruby and Daniella what Miguel had said.

"Don't worry about it," they told me. "Just forget about it."

But I couldn't forget.

Things got worse. Our friend Akilah came up to us and said, "Happiness! Did you forget that this was Picture Day?"

I looked around and realized that my friends were all wearing their favorite clothes. I was just wearing my school uniform. *Oh no!* Now I felt as if a bunch of worms had started dancing in my stomach.

That afternoon, while we were in line for the pictures, another friend, Julia, comforted me.

"Nobody cares if you have a bad hairstyle," she said. "Don't worry about it."

When I was in front of the camera, I wanted to put my hands up and cover my hair. But the photographer and her helper wouldn't let me. They told me to smile, so I smiled. Sort of.

Luckily, for the rest of that week no one teased me about that hairstyle.

And I found two ways to make things better.

Number one, I took in what my friends had told me: *Don't worry. Just let it go.*

Number two, on Saturday I got permission to use the computer at home, and I searched online to find a hairstyle I liked. I asked Mama to fix my hair that way, and she did. Now we do this every weekend.

Mama is really very talented with hair.

The Horse (Panasonic Lumix TS25)
Alana-Jain Feder, 11
Long Beach, CA

Oscar

After a fire burns his family farm and orchard—their livelihood—
Oscar and his siblings must find work

By Brennan Cameron, 10
Newtown, CT

"Come on!" Oscar yelled to his younger brother, Finn. Finn ran to catch up. "Of all the fires in the world, why did one have to come here?" Oscar complained.

"I don't know," replied Finn, skipping along.

Finn was seven and did not like to work hard. He preferred fishing with Oscar in the river nearby.

Oscar sighed and looked around. His family's farm and apple orchard had been burned by a forest fire. Luckily, the rain came before the barn, animals, and house had been lost. About ninety percent of the food they needed to survive the winter had been destroyed, and all of their apples were gone. They had none left to sell. A lot of the trees on the Ozark Mountains near their farm had also burned.

It was a beautiful day outside, but nobody was in any mood to enjoy it. Today was the first day Oscar had gone outside to explore since the fire. Everybody in the family was trying to figure out ways to earn money. His sister, Ava, was going to sell lace. Ava was bossy, two years older than Oscar, and liked to help her mom

take care of the house. His mom was going to make candles using beeswax from the nearby hives, and his father was already gone looking for a job, having heard there were jobs near the railroad. Oscar wondered if anybody needed help caring for their crops or animals.

Walking down to the town, the boys talked about how much the fire had damaged the forest.

"Why did the fire burn the good stuff and not the outhouse?" joked Finn.

Their outhouse was a piece of junk on the edge of their property. The roof was caving in, the door would not close, and it smelled really, really bad. Everybody was afraid to go in there because it might cave in and they would fall into who knows what.

Oscar was silent.

After the long walk to town, Oscar really hoped they could find somebody who needed help. All day long they went around asking, but nobody had any jobs for two small boys. They asked the rancher, the minister, and even Mr. Johnson, who was smoking a pipe on his porch. They could not find any way to make money. When they returned home, they found that mother had made seven candles and Ava had sewed quite a lot of lace. Finn went fishing, and Oscar shuffled into the barn to visit his best friend, Rose.

Oscar walked immediately to Rose, his foal, and hugged her tightly. He told her what was happening. Rose seemed to understand, and she gave a sad whine. Rose was his favorite animal on the planet. Oscar had helped his father deliver her, which had been so exciting. He had taken care of Rose ever since.

Whenever something was worrying him, he confided in her. It made him feel better to have someone understand his pain. After Oscar talked to Rose, he usually felt better, but today he was still sad. He fed the other horses, the milk cow, and their five chickens. He collected the eggs for his brother because he knew Finn would not be home to do it. Oscar returned to Rose and nuzzled her some more as he wondered how he could help his family. When he noticed that it was getting dark, he said goodbye to Rose and walked slowly to the house with a grim expression on his face.

Oscar slumped into the house and took his favorite seat near the toasty fireplace. Oscar's father had built the fireplace out of fieldstones taken from the farm, and sitting there made Oscar think of his father.

His mother came over to him, and he told her that he had not found a job.

He felt useless and sad. His mother comforted him by rubbing his back and saying everything would work out. He was not sure if everything would, but it was nice to hear.

He walked across the creaky floorboards to his bed. The bed creaked and groaned under his weight. When Finn got in later, the mattress sagged even further. Oscar lay in bed thinking even after he could hear Finn snoring.

Oscar woke to the chirping of the birds. He did his chores, ate a piece of bread with a glass of milk, and headed back to town to try again. He was still hungry, and he heard his belly rumble. Again he went through the same routine of offering his help and getting rejected. Oscar sat down on a bench. Two men nearby were talking about horses, and Oscar leaned in to listen more closely. Mr. Johnson needed a new horse because his old one had passed away. He wanted a gentle horse for his carriage. Mr. Murphy mentioned he would let him know if he heard of any horses for sale.

Oscar thought about this, and he got an idea. Oscar's family had two more horses, Blazer and Bessie. Blazer was gentle and graceful while Bessie was prone to kicking. He walked back home pondering the man's request deeply. Oscar believed that if they could sell Blazer, everything would be just right. By the time Oscar got home, he could already taste the delicious food his family would be eating this winter.

Oscar sprinted into the kitchen and breathlessly announced his genius plan to his mom. Sadly, his sister heard it too, and she yelled, "You can't do that—he is the family horse. You can't sell Blazer!"

Oscar looked at his mom and she sighed. "Oh, honey. Blazer is needed to pull the carriage and work in the fields."

"Rose can take his place. Rose would do well in the fields," Oscar argued.

"Rose would take too long to train, and Blazer is the only one Bessie does not kick," Mom replied, showing Oscar a recent hoof mark on her leg.

"Told you so." Ava laughed.

Oscar stomped out the door without closing it while his mom scolded Ava for interrupting her conversation with Oscar.

Oscar was so upset he ran right into the barn to tell Rose. His feelings rushed out like a cheetah chasing its prey. He confided everything, like how Mom would not let him sell Blazer and how they would not have enough money or food for the winter.

Oscar saddled Rose for a walk to calm himself. Rose walked slowly to make the ride comfortable for Oscar. As they moved across the property, Oscar was reminded of the damage the fire had done.

Rose led the way. Oscar barely felt a bump at all!

Later, when he unsaddled Rose, he realized Rose had been trying to tell him something all along. She was trying to tell him that she was gentle.

Oscar put that idea out of his mind immediately because he adored Rose.

He could never imagine selling her. He could never imagine not seeing her beautiful face every day or telling her his deepest secrets. He trudged up the hill to the house, full of gloom.

Oscar felt depleted when he awoke the next morning. There was barely food for breakfast. Even though he forbade himself from thinking about selling Rose, he thought about it anyway. He thought about what his life would be like without the beautiful face of Rose looking at him every day. He would feel terrible and miss her greatly.

Dinner was a piece of stale bread with a few carrots and potatoes. They also had a few small fish Finn had caught. It did not feel like it was enough.

Oscar slept in the barn because he could not fall asleep with Finn snoring so loudly. When Oscar woke up, Rose was cuddling right beside him, deep in sleep. As he pet Rose, she nuzzled him and licked his face. Oscar knew that Rose trusted him to do the right thing.

All of a sudden, he knew what he was going to do. He was going to sell Rose. He slowly walked to the house to tell his mom.

Oscar burst into the door looking for his mother. "I'm going to sell Rose," he announced.

Mom whispered, "Are you sure you want to do that, honey? You love her. You don't have to sell her. We would never make you sell your horse. You know we will find some way to get the farm back and running."

"Mom I have to. It will help the family, and Rose trusts me to do the right thing."

Mom sighed. "Honey, I can make more candles. Dad will come back with money. Ava will . . ."

"I want to, Mom," Oscar insisted. "My mind is made up."

Mom hugged him and brushed hair away from his eyes. "You know what is best." She smiled and kissed him on the cheek. She watched Oscar walk out the door while trying to hide her tears.

Oscar rode Rose to town with mixed feelings about his decision. He was crying and beginning to regret his choice. He tried to talk to Rose and tell her that everything was going to be okay and that Mr. Johnson was a very nice man. Rose walked as slow as a snail, and yet they still arrived sooner than expected. He sat on the bench with Rose next to him and thought about all of the adventures they'd had and all of the times he had confided his deepest secrets to her. But he knew that if he did not sell Rose, his family and the animals might starve. They would have trouble starting their farm up again. At least Rose would be taken care of.

Oscar and Rose walked along the dusty dirt road to Mr. Johnson's home. When he arrived, Oscar waited outside and told himself that everything was going to be alright. Before Oscar had a chance to knock, the door opened and Mrs. Johnson stood in the doorway.

Oscar asked to see Mr. Johnson, and Mrs. Johnson said that he was out back.

"Thank you," replied Oscar.

As he walked behind the house, Oscar found Mr. Johnson smoking his pipe on a blue rocking chair. Oscar approached Mr. Johnson with Rose by his side.

"Hello, Mr. Johnson." Oscar smiled.

"Hello, Oscar," replied Mr. Johnson. "What can I do for you?"

"I have come to offer this beautiful, gentle, one-of-a-kind horse," Oscar proudly stated.

"Yes!" Mr. Johnson exclaimed. "Finally, somebody is offering me a horse!"

He was so happy he did not notice the sullen expressions on their faces. Out of the blue, Oscar started crying.

"What's wrong, Oscar?" asked Mr. Johnson gently.

With tears streaming down his cheeks, Oscar told Mr. Johnson how much he loved Rose and how much they had been through together.

"Then why do you want to sell your horse?" Mr. Johnson asked.

Oscar told him about the fire, how they had lost all of their apple trees and crops, and how they needed to get money. When he finished, he hugged Rose tightly.

Mr. Johnson saw the connection between the two, and he thought for a while. "This horse is pretty young," he said. "I don't know if I could train Rose to pull my carriage. It would be very hard for a man my age to go through that."

Oscar's hopes were crushed.

"I would need someone to help me take care of Rose," he continued.

Oscar's face lit up the sky. "I could do that!" he exclaimed. "Every day I could come to your place and work with Rose. I could feed her, clean out her stall, and brush her. I would love to do that!"

"I could only pay you 50 cents a week," replied Mr. Johnson. "And I would need to have you work with Rose every day."

Oscar was so happy he hugged the surprised Mr. Johnson. "I'll take it!"

They worked out the details, and then Oscar led Rose to the stable. He prepared her bed and let her know he would be back the next day and every day after that to see her.

Then he hugged her, a warm, fuzzy kind of hug. The kind of hug that said, "See you tomorrow" instead of "Goodbye."

Victoria (Samsung Galaxy S9+)
Joey Vasaturo, 10
Colebrook, CT

The Trials and Tribulations of Swifty Appledoe (Part Three)

By Ariana Kralicek, 12
Auckland, New Zealand

This is the third and final installment of Ariana Kralicek's novella. You can read the first two installments in the April and May 2021 issues of Stone Soup, *or in its entirety online.*

Chapter 17

On the way to the hospital, everything is like a jumble. It kind of feels like sorting through old books, if you know what I mean. There are the ones you love, ones you hate, and ones you can't even remember reading.

Like now. We're speeding along the streets, Grandma at the wheel and me yelling, "Go, go, go!"

I hate that it's uncertain about how Mum and my brother are. I haven't heard anything about them yet. And I can't remember what happened at school. It's like it was one of those dreams you can't think about after it's over because you've forgotten.

Finally, we arrive at the Auckland Hospital.

"Hurry, Grandma!" I impatiently beg as she unloads bags upon bags of gifts.

She asks me to carry some for her. I do. They probably weigh at least several kilograms, but they feel as light as feathers to me.

We race inside the main building,

Grandma briskly walking and me pulling her along crazily. When we get to the reception desk, the lady sitting behind it stares at us boredly. *How is she not excited?! This is so weird! Ugh, Swifty. Snap out of it!*

"Purpose of visit?" she blandly asks.

"Grace McClean!" My grandma's dentures nearly fly out of her mouth. She's really excited.

"Okay. That's level seven, ward three," she replies.

We hurry over to the elevator. I jab repeatedly at the button going up, while Grandma smiles at me, stressed but bursting with excitement, her foot tapping on the hard floor. Oh boy!

The elevator finally arrives, and we race inside. I jab at the level-seven button, and slowly but surely, we go up.

"H-hurry, hurry, hurry," I whisper. "H-hurry, hurry, h-h-hurry."

Ding! The elevator doors roll open. Grandma wobbles out, a big smile plastered on her face.

"Ward three—there it is!" she

shrieks cheerily.

But just as we're about to go in, I feel a terrible nervous pang in my stomach. My throat squeezes shut in panic. I feel like I can't breathe. I grip my grandmother's hand tightly, feeling the map of her life stretched across her wrinkled palm.

"Hey, sweetie. It's okay to feel nervous," she says gently. "Why don't we just go inside. You can hide behind me if you want to!" She grins cheekily. "Now smile!"

I stretch my lips into a fake grin. She nods, and clasping hands, we walk inside. The room is dim and grey.

My mum is on a big hospital bed, cradling a tiny lump. My dad walks over to us and gives me and Grandma a big hug.

"Come on, Swifty," he whispers. He sounds quite emotional, but I suppose it IS one of those kinds of situations.

I go over and sit on the edge of my mum's bed. There's a drip going into her, but nothing is actually that scary.

"Swifty, meet your baby brother," my mum whispers. And then suddenly my hand is stroking my brother.

O. M. G.

He's so warm and tiny, wrapped up in cozy pale-blue blankets. He's silent, but he's making little tuts as he sleeps. Thin wisps of hair frame his chubby cheeks. And his little pinched face . . . *Ughh, soooo cute.*

No matter what happens, I'm going to do whatever it takes to protect him. This is the moment I want to last forever.

I lie on the thin air mattress my grandma set up for me. I need to stay with her until tomorrow because my mum needs to rest at the hospital.

Don't get me wrong: I love my grandma, but I really want to be in my own homey bedroom instead of trying to sleep in the nearly empty, dim spare room in her small house.

I check the time on the digital clock propped beside me. It reads 12:01 a.m. I need to get to sleep. Tomorrow are the student council elections, and I have to be wide awake for that. But I can't seem to shut my eyes. I'm worried about my brother. *What if something happens to him in the night? If he gets sick? If the next day he's given to the wrong people after a test?*

I squeeze my eyelids closed and for the hundredth time try to fall asleep, telling myself that the people at the hospital know what they're doing, that he was fine when I saw him, and that my mum will keep him safe.

Chapter 18

It's the day of the student council tryouts. I squirm nervously in my seat, just like at the concerta and while in the car on the way to my first (and last) ballet class.

My hands clench sweatily around my cue cards (which are ripped because of my impulsive gripping, just like they clenched the scissors when I cut off nearly all of my hair), and I can't stop my teeth from chattering like when my baby brother was born.

I can handle this.

Mrs. Mulberry bounces into class.

"Good morning, first of all," she exclaims, placing her books on her desk. "And secondly, could all of the students trying out for the role of our class councilor please stand up and go outside? Write your names on the board before you go, though," she adds with a smile.

Mrs. Mulberry loves the student council tryouts. Rumor has it she loves it more than watching *Keeping Up With the Kardashians*.

I stand up and shuffle over to the door. I can hear my classmates gossiping. Especially about me. Someone holds the door open, and I quietly walk through. I hear it click shut, and then I look up.

Oh . . . kay.

All of the popular kids in my class are pacing around in circles or biting their lips, fiddling with their hair or encouraging each other.

I see Luke O'Connor rehearsing weird flirty glances that make him look like he's constipated, Tyler Peterson waving to a massive crowd of his imaginary fans, Hamish Clonestar admiring his tiny muscles, Brooke tetchily rolling her judgmental eyes, Amy Ryan looking picture perfect mouthing out her speech, and Stella Chichester-Clark grinning smugly. Again.

Mrs. Mulberry minces out of the room and calls us all over. We nervously crowd around her. I end up at the edge.

"Now, you guys—I just want every one of you to know that you are all winners, no matter what happens."

I roll my eyes undetectably. It's the dreaded reassurance of the teacher.

Deep down, I'm pretty sure Mrs. Mulberry knows how bad her pep talks are, but she's probably signed

some kind of teacher contract saying she has to give them.

"So . . ." She presents a piece of paper and a pen. "Who wants to go first?"

Tyler Peterson shoves his hand up into the air like he's holding a toy airplane and wants to see how high he can reach. Mrs. Mulberry scribbles his name down. Amy Ryan goes second, then Luke, then Hamish, then Brooke, Stella, and finally, me.

I mean, last is okay, but by then everybody's bored. I lean against the corridor wall and cup my hands around my left ear, but I can only hear the muffled speeches of each contestant.

Most of the girls giggle at Tyler, glare jealously at Amy, blush at Luke, swoon at Hamish, and smile at Stella. Nearly all the boys only pay attention to their friends. Typical.

All the candidates have emerged from the classroom, grinning with satisfaction.

It's my turn to head in. I slowly open the door a crack, allowing myself to see just a thin line of my class. The air from inside the room cools my face.

I can do this.

"Now let's give it up for SWIFTY!" Mrs. Mulberry announces as I stand at the center of the class.

I open my mouth wide open, only to hear Brooke mutter, "Fish." I don't know how, but I can still hear her through the door. I mentally shut off my ears from the world and begin to speak.

"Hi! As you already know, my name is Swifty. I'd like to run for our class councilor this year because I

As I make my way outside the classroom so the votes can be taken, I start to hyperventilate.

believe that we need a change. I think that I am honest, responsible, and I work hard. But this isn't about me. It's about YOU.

"As you know, we don't have a lot of school clubs at the moment, yet there are so many things to do online, with coding and more available at our fingertips. I propose that we start up an ICT club for those of you that like coding or games.

"Another thing: there are those of us who . . . who find it hard to make friends, myself included. I think that maybe we could all help each other to make some friends, because no one deserves to be alone. Or hurt in any way." I stare straight at Brooke through the window in the front door.

She leers right back at me, but I'm imagining her internally blushing.

"Thank you," I conclude.

A burst of applause shatters my eardrums.

Oh. M.G. This is what it feels like to be accepted.

As I make my way outside the classroom so the votes can be taken, I start to hyperventilate. There just isn't enough oxygen. I heave and lean against the wall. My throat feels sore, like I've just swallowed chips. My legs feel like I'm learning to surf for the first time.

I gather myself together and glance at the other contestants. They seem more relaxed now that they've done their speeches, but of course everyone is anticipating the final results. It's kind of like an eating contest. Once you've shoveled down

most of the food, you feel satisfied— but when you look at the plate and see all that food still waiting to be eaten, you wonder if you'll ever accomplish the feat you've been aiming for.

Stella looks pretty chill, which makes me nervous. I think she knows the outcome: she and Brooke.

I bite my lip. *Will it be like the last tryouts, where she won yet again?*

Just as I start to ponder whether the elections are rigged (I mean, no one even looks that happy when Stella wins), the classroom door creaks open and Mrs. Mulberry's head peeks out from the doorframe.

"Come on in, guys." She grins excitedly.

Luke, Hamish, Tyler, and Amy head in first, followed by Stella, Brooke, and me. We're told to line up at the front of the class.

Great. Standing in front of twenty other people is not my cup of tea, even though my ambition WAS to stand in front of many more.

Is there something on my chin? I wonder. I bow my head down and quickly swipe at my mouth with the sleeve of my jersey. Nope, nothing's there.

I stare at the ground, and then remember that if I do that it'll look like I'm unfit for the role. I remember a trick Dad taught me once where instead of staring at the people you're talking to, you stare just above their heads, basically at the wall. I tilt my eyes upward and take slow, deep breaths. I think I've done okay.

"Okay, everyone. So, I've counted

the votes and now I will announce the results," Mrs. Mulberry announces. "But first . . ." She pauses, like she's about to give a really big speech.

"I've said this many times before, and I will say it again: you are all winners." I cringe.

Inner me is literally screaming for the results. *Hurry up!* I think.

"So the runner up, and also the standby, is Swifty!" Mrs. Mulberry exclaims, like even she can't believe it.

Wait. ME?

"And the winner is, of course, Stella." Mrs. Mulberry gleams.

Stella and I are called up to the front, and we each get a Crunchie Bar.

Wow.

Brooke stares at me scornfully as I make my way back to my seat.

I tear open the glossy Crunchie Bar wrapping and pop the bar into my mouth.

I did it.

"The first meeting is today at lunchtime in the staff room, girls," Mrs. Mulberry states. "For this meeting, both of you will be attending, just to get the hang of things and all that."

Stella shifts her gaze to me and raises her eyebrows. I give her a nod and close my eyes. I just realized that I have to work with her.

Chapter 19

As the lunchtime moving bell rings, I hurriedly pack away my lunch so I can make my way up to the staff room.

The staff room is considered gold by the Year Ones and Twos. It's for the teachers, and only certain students are allowed in it. If you ever get to go there, you know you're lucky.

I race up the stairs, trying not to make too much of a thumping noise as I rush up. When I finally reach the top, I glance around the spacious room.

At one end is a kitchen for the teachers. There's an island with a polished white surface, but you can't see much of it because of the mountains of plates piled on top of it and in the small sink. Behind it is a mini fridge, stove, oven, and microwave. To the left of that are several cubbies with name tags. I glance to my left. There are dozens of chairs set up in a square-like pattern, and in between the chairs are small tables with educational magazines resting on the glassy surfaces. There's a whiteboard at one end with a few sentences scrawled on it. The principal is standing in front of it.

And there are the student councilors.

A wave of awkwardness, if that's even a thing, hits me. They all look different, but still the same: ironed outfits, good skin, cleanly cut and gelled hair.

The one word that could describe them all in a hot second would be "perfect."

I look down at what I'm wearing: baggy khaki shorts and an old pink T-shirt. My jumper's tied around my waist kind of loosely, like a little kid clinging onto their mother as she says goodbye. Okay, that was a weird example, but still . . .

"Oh, hello Swifty!" Principal Fintan greets me. The councilors' heads turn. *Oh no.* I shyly stare down at my shoes.

"Stella unfortunately couldn't join us today. I think she had a one-off event to attend—but anyway, would you like to come over and join our conversation?"

It's a rhetorical question. I make my way over to a spare seat and sink deep down into its cushiony depths.

"Now, where was I? Oh, yes. Tom, what were you saying?" They even have ordinary names. No hate to the Toms out there or anything, but . . .

"I just feel like . . . nearly all of us"— he gestures to the student council, noticeably excluding me—"are being left out. I mean, the other students"— he waves a hand at me—just don't try hard enough." Right. Thick clouds of heat swirl around my face and my stomach pangs. "Like, we're in the student council because we're better. I feel like she"—gestures—"doesn't deserve to be a part of our council. And . . ." *Blah blah blah.* I tune out. It's not worth listening, and what point is Tom even trying to make?

"Err, thank you, Tom." Principal Fintan winces but hides it with an appreciative nod. "And just a quick tip: make sure what you're saying doesn't offend others. If it does, then you can talk about it privately to me or just keep it to yourself."

"Now Swifty, what do you have to say about this?"

"Erm, I think that what Tom says doesn't make a lot of sense to me. I mean, of course there are students who do try or want to try but who are more introverted or need help with things . . . but why does that even matter?"

Hmm.

"Tom, how would you feel about being teased every day?" I say.

He sighs. "Uhh . . . not that good, I guess."

"Exactly. A certain someone has been making fun of me, in fact, since Year Four. And because of that I shut down. And I'm also super average. But now what I'm trying to do is become like that person's friend so I can be better."

Principal Fintan gives me a strange look.

Another guy whose name I don't know gives me another look. "But you're fine just the way you are, I guess. Well, other than not trying enough at school."

That was blunt.

"Be yourself: everyone else is already taken," Abigail from Room Four quips.

"That's Oscar Wilde," someone whose voice is very, very, very familiar pipes up.

Oh no. Linda? I stare at her in shock. *What's she doing here?* She gives me an uncertain smile, then looks away. I can see her hands fiddling, fingers twisting to make weird shapes. But then, a thumbs up. I smile internally. I've been forgiven. We may not be friends anymore, but at least now she doesn't have a lasting grudge.

Others start to throw inspirational quotes my way, and I'm lost for a moment. Then it hits me: All along, I've been trying to be like Stella so I could have the same amount of recognition she had and so everyone, or at least nearly everyone, would like me. But throughout all the terms I've been doing this, I've been discovering my own talents.

From learning the violin, I found out I'm a really good drummer. From attempting ballet, I've found out that hip-hop may be more suited to me. Because I cut my hair, I've discovered some of my tastes. When my baby brother was born, I recognized that maybe I do need some help with the twisty topic of friends. And through making it into the student council, I've discovered myself—after all, I've just had an epiphany for the first time.

Is that an achievement?

All I know is that for the rest of the day, I feel a huge sense of relief.

Chapter 20

"Hello, sweetheart!" my mum exclaims blissfully.

She's sitting on the soft, carpeted lounge floor, playing with my brother. He's lying on his tummy and wriggling around. I giggle and drop my bag by the doorway, carefully heel- and-toeing, then crouching down.

My brother's face is really chubby, and he's drooling heaps. His hands look like tiny balloons, fingers curled delicately. I sit down and gently pick him up, placing him on my lap. His eyes stare up at me curiously, like he's reading my mind and knows more than you'd think. My brother grasps my index finger. His hands are moist and warm. I wrinkle my nose, still smiling, as I think of the reason behind the moisture. A question pops into my head.

"Mum," I ask as I look up at her. "What's my brother's name?"

"To be honest, your dad and I haven't really decided yet," she says, brushing strands of hair out of her eyes.

"I'll go look at some," I offer.

I get up, placing my brother gently back on the ground, then walk out the door and down the corridor toward the office.

I sit down in front of the computer and type "names for boys." The first names that come up are

- Kane.
- Noah.
- William.
- James.
- Luke.
- Arthur.
- Benjamin.
- Mason.
- Lewis.

The first thought that comes to mind is that these names would definitely not suit my brother. I click on the website that featured them to see what other names there are and scroll down.

- Jayden.
- Thomas.
- Harrison.
- Finlay.
- Zane.
- Zachary.
- Clayton.
- Grayson.

Yet again, none of these names suit my brother. I go out of the site and try a different one.

- Charles.
- James.
- Gareth.
- Claude.
- Dagwood.
- Zenith.

I stop scrolling down. Zenith. That sounds nice. I leave that site and search the name. The definition is "the highest point."

I smile.

My baby brother, in the end, made me happy. And my parents. At our highest point. I hare out of the room and scream, "Zenith! Mum, my brother's name is Zenith!"

Chapter 21

This year, it feels like each day is more significant than the last, each one a day where I tried out for something. So I'm not going to say, "It's the day of the . . ." I've already said that way too many times.

So, I guess I'll start with this: I slump boredly in an auditorium seat as I wait unenthusiastically for the annual student awards to start.

There's a stage, black floor matted with small globs of chewing gum from the theater kids who didn't pay attention to the rules. Rows upon rows of red seats are stacked on top of one another, like an amphitheater. It feels like one. Halfway up, a glass barrier separates them from a differently designed row of seats that look like rugged stairs. The walls are a dark blue, and a large sculpture of the school logo has been hung up on one.

Many of the students and parents are wearing fancy clothes. I'm wearing a mint-green "jumpsuit" (sparkly top and leggings, to be exact) and silver boots because if we have to run for it for some reason, I want to be the first person out of there.

I know it's going to be the usual people who win the awards. The sporty ones, the smart ones, the perfect ones. Call me a bad sport, but I reckon if you were sitting through the same thing year after year, you would feel the same way too.

The others in my class have similar expressions as mine; the only difference is that they've got friends to talk to about it.

Principal Fintan taps the mic, briefly standing center stage. "Quiet, everyone." His voice echoes throughout the auditorium. The chatter steadily draws to a close.

I spot my parents sitting in the back left corner. They give me a small, tired wave—my brother, Zenith, has been keeping them and me up all night—my dad making Zenith's hand move in an arc too.

"Good morning, students. And welcome, parents," Principal Fintan begins. His voice sounds foreign and serious in the microphone, but a beaming smile is plastered across his face.

"The annual Bellmore Primary School Awards are just about to begin; in order for that to happen, parents, could you please turn off any devices you have brought with you."

There's a small murmur as reluctant parents bring out their phones and tap some things into them before putting them back into their pockets or bags.

Principal Fintan waits for the noise to die out and then actually begins. My teacher said the awards would probably last about two hours. My stomach grumbles even though I don't feel hungry. Principal Fintan starts to speak again.

"We have so many talented students at Bellmore. The sheer amount of genius young minds and driven people here is extraordinary. Sadly, we cannot hand out awards to everyone. So, the awards we are handing out today will be going to those in the student body who have excelled at different areas, either in the curriculum or in extracurricular activities.

"We will begin with the class awards, then move on to the extracurriculars and sport, and then to the students who have shown promise in certain subjects, and finally . . . to the Bellmore pupil of the year.

"So, could I please have the Year One teachers come down to the front."

Click, thump, thump, click. Teachers in flowery skirts and woolen vests hurry down the stairs nimbly. When they reach the bottom, they're handed a slim pile of beige certificates each.

Room Twenty's teacher goes first.

"Connor." Her voice is light and fluffy, like candyfloss clouds.

An arrogant-looking boy gets up from his cramped-looking seat and carefully walks down the steps to the front. He's dressed in a full-on suit, his hair parted and gelled heavily. When he reaches the stage, he waves to his parents. They smile and wave back. I reckon they might've told the boy he was going to win an award beforehand, because his reaction is just a small wry smile.

"Alexandria."

A small girl wearing a very poofy rainbow dress bounces out of her seat and skips down the steps, her lips stretched to breaking point. Her reaction when she's handed the certificate is priceless.

Names upon names are called. The line of boys and girls coming down to receive the awards seems endless. It feels like an age before the Year Fours are called down to get theirs.

Next, the extracurricular people are called down to receive their awards. Stella gains her fifth award, which I didn't even know was possible.

I start to squirm in my seat. My legs and back are cramping up, and my mouth is wet with saliva. I'm starting to feel thirsty.

I notice other people starting to look like they feel the same way too, so it's amazing when Principal Fintan finally announces that we can all exit the hall for an intermission to stretch our legs and grab a quick drink of water.

As soon as I can, I literally bounce out of my seat and race down the stairs. I. Need. Water.

I'm one of the first ones to the water fountain. I open my mouth and a stream of H2O floods in.

Mmmmm.

I continue to suck desperately at the water as it runs down my sore throat. By the time I've put off nearly everyone from taking a sip, I feel as though I've swallowed a grandfather clock. Well, maybe not a grandfather clock. Let's say a tiny chair.

I return to my seat, satisfactorily plopping down in it just in time for the remaining awards.

Best Sportsman. Best Sportswoman. Most Creative Person. Future in STEM. Dux. Most Potential. On and on the awards go. All handed to perfect-looking people, including

Stella. She seems to be getting even more than usual.

Then, finally, it's the Student of the Year Award.

It's going to be Stella. Principal Fintan has the same smile on his face, the one he always does. Mrs. Mulberry has that look too.

Principal Fintan is just about to start announcing the Student of the Year (Stella) when all of a sudden, I get a wave of urgency signaling to me from my bladder.

Oh no. I regret drinking so much water.

Actually, take that away:

I doubly regret drinking so much water.

All eyes are trained on the stage, which is exactly where the exit is. If I get up from my seat to answer Mother Nature's call, everyone will see me.

I squirm.

Do it, do it, do it, my mind whispers eagerly.

I glance at Mrs. Mulberry and make the toilet sign with my hands. She shakes her head and smiles a very strange smile.

WHAT?!

"This Student of the Year award goes to someone who has stepped out of their comfort zone," Principal Fintan says. "They have participated in many extracurricular activities, including ballet and music, as well as becoming a part of the student council. They even made it into the news!"

I tune in. I already know it's going to be Stella, but I need to distract myself from you know what.

"In the past, they have struggled to try new things and were, I quote,

'super average.'"

I cringe on the inside. *No way can it be Stella. She would never say that about herself. I really pity the person who did say that about themselves, though. They must be super embarrassed right now, especially since they're being singled out from about 600 others.*

"This year, they even tried to be more like one of their peers." *Oh my gosh. Whoever the Student of the Year is, they must be feeling doubly humiliated.*

"But because of that, they have grown and become their own person. And I think it's very fitting that on their last year of primary school they'll get a milestone award."

Okay. I'm feeling better about the whole situation. It's actually not as urgent as I thought it was. Maybe. Just a few more minutes, Swifty, and you're all done.

"So with that being said, I will now announce the Student of the Year. She likes to go by her nickname, but I think I'll announce her by her real one. The Student of the Year is . . . drumroll everyone . . ."

I join in with the rest of the school and the parents. For each drumbeat, most people in the school will probably be thinking, *Who is it?* But instead, I'm thinking, *I really need to go. I really need to go.*

"Zendaya Appledoe!"

That poor person. They must really be peeing their pants right now, like I'm about to.

But then why are my classmates patting my back and saying, "Well done!" and, "Good on you. We really needed a change," And why is Stella smiling her first humble smile in what, in my opinion, seems to be since the day she was born?

Why is my teacher holding my cold, shaky hand as I stumble down the auditorium steps, my legs wobbling like jelly on a cake? And why can I hear my parents screaming and clapping above everyone else, saying encouragingly, "Go for it, Swifty!" Why am I walking toward Principal Fintan on my own? And why is he shaking my hand and handing me a heavy, sparkling bronze trophy?

"Congratulations, Swifty," he says, handing the microphone over to me. "Would you like to say anything?"

"Umm. . ." I glance at my parents and baby brother. "I'd like to dedicate this to my baby brother, because I want him to grow up proud of who he is. And obviously my parents."

My tummy feels like it's doing grand jetés. Is this a dream? And then suddenly, Mother Nature calls yet again.

I whisper something in Principal Fintan's ear and looks like he's going to laugh, but he nods.

And then I'm racing out of there, cold surprise curling around my mind.

Chapter 22

What just happened?!

My parents snap photos of me on their phones as I hold the gleaming school trophy. Dozens of names have been etched onto its surface, dating back to the 1930s, which is amazing.

I've only just realized this, but history is in my hands. Of course, I don't get to keep it. But that's okay. I'm still coming to grips with how I even won the trophy in the first place. I mean, how have I been chosen out of over 600 people? Stella should have gotten it. Right?

The noisy chatter of parents and teachers deafens me. My parents smile.

"I can't believe you did it, Swifty!" My dad grins from ear to ear as he gets into another picture with me.

My mum smiles. "Looks like one of your friends is joining us."

I turn around and see none other than Stella Chichester-Clark clacking toward me, her designer high heels clicking against the ground.

"Hey, Swifty!" she says, flicking her long, golden hair back from her face. She brushes her slightly poofy dress, nails painted a cherry blossom pink. The dress is mint green just like my jumpsuit. Well, leggings and a top.

I paste a small smile onto my face, like I would if I photoshopped a photo on a computer. *What is Stella going to say?*

"I just wanted to let you know . . . well done on winning Student of the Year." She congratulates me, now twirling a lock of her hair around one of her clean fingers.

I don't know what to say. Stella's nice, but she doesn't say congratulations very often. A smile spreads across my face before I can control it.

"Umm, thank you. Congrats to you too." She grins.

"Hey, this'll sound kinda random, but can we be friends?" *Hang on. Stella asked me to be her friend?!*

"It's just that . . . I've noticed you've been copying me all year, and I thought that maybe . . . you wanted to hang out?"

Uh oh. This is super embarrassing. She knew all along while I was trying to keep it a secret.

"Err, sorry ab-b-bout th-that," I stutter. I always speak funny when I'm nervous, which is kind of annoying.

"It's fine. I knew you wanted to be just like me all along."

I gasp in shock. That was so rude! Stella never—

"It's a joke, Swifty! Your expression . . . I know you would never do that." I cringe inside my head. *If only you knew, Stella. If only you knew.*

"Swifty, we've got to go now," my mum whispers. She and Dad give me a quick hug and kiss before waving goodbye.

Almost a second after that, Brooke appears from the crowd, Karen dragging her along like a child with an oversized doll.

Karen pushes Brooke in front of me. "Brooke," she snaps. "Say it."

Karen hasn't talked like that since dinosaurs ruled the Earth. She's normally quiet and obliging.

"Mm, sorry," Brooke mumbles.

"Sorry who?" Karen inquires.

"SWIFTY! Sorry, Swifty!" Brooke yells. She storms off, Karen trailing somewhat tiredly behind and waving to me. "Well done, Swifty!"

I smile anxiously. It feels weird that I'm getting so many compliments. But I brush the feeling off and turn back to Stella.

"Yes. Let's be friends," I answer her question confidently.

Epilogue

I feel like a lot of people say similar things to this, but I'm still going to say it too.

If you had asked me a few years ago to hang out with Stella every day, I would have said, "No way, José." But here I am, sitting on a bench with Stella as we snack on our lunch, watching kids play rugby and hang from monkey bars.

It's our first year of high school, and so far it's going pretty well.

My brother, Zenith, has just turned three, which means he's toddling around the house a lot. But he made up for it by saying his first word, my name: Zendaya.

Speaking of which, I'm not going by the nickname Swifty anymore. It's like an old T-shirt I've grown out of.

I haven't made any other new friends just yet, but Stella's forced me to join the writing club at school, so I at least hang out with others. I think I'm actually okay at writing. Maybe.

If you had asked me what I thought of Stella a few years ago, I would've said, "Princessy, perfect, annoying."

But if you look at her now, her blonde hair is slowly turning brown, and she's actually quite disorganized.

"You can't be perfect at everything," she said one day after getting a D+ in art. I giggled and playfully shoved her away.

So I guess the moral of the story that I'm leaving you with is: "Don't judge a book by its cover." And if you've quickly flicked through to the very end of the book you're holding in your very hands right now, you shouldn't be either.

But if you are, I still suggest you give this a try. Yes, there's a cheesy ending, and yes, very clichéd, but yes, you should read it.

And this sounds kinda random, but...

People can change. You can change. Your view on books can change. iPhones can change. Towers, parks, and even countries can change.

And that's what this book is about. Change.

Highlights from Stonesoup.com

From Stone Soup Writing Workshop #17: Writing about Music

The Writing Challenge
Use any musical element—different instruments, arrangements, styles, and settings—to write about music. It could be about how music makes someone feel, or the story of someone involved in music, or anything else you think up.

An excerpt from
"My Brother Was the Bayou"
By Liam Hancock, 12
Danville, CA

"I want to listen to the man tonight," I said nonchalantly, leaning back in my rocking chair. I glanced over to Mama, who seemed a world away. With needles, and thread, and tablecloths strewn about tables.

She sighed, her fingers artfully dancing around one another in a timeless ballet. Needle, thread, tablecloth. Tablecloth, needle, thread. "If Pops is in the mood," she replied, her voice distant as the indigo sky spanned out about the swaying trees and warming bayou air. A small, wooden raft trundled by. "And it's up to the man, Jackson, if he wants to play."

I shrugged, grabbing hold of our shambled roof and yanking myself to a stand, nodding in satisfaction as the rocking chair rolled back and slammed headlong into our small swamp cabin, sending the precarious boards shuddering in protest. I leapt down to the muddy banks, swatting away an assault of mosquitoes.

"He plays when I want him to," I pressed, the brown-greenish sheen of river water and soppy dirt seeping into my hunting boots. "And when I want to sleep, he stops." I hesitated. "I think he likes me."

Mama took a pretty second to cast me a quizzical look. "That's the most fine dandy and rediculous idea I've ever heard with these two ears." She returned back to her knitting. "Pops should be nearby, maybe on Elkdead Island. Why don't you take the skiff over?"

I grinned. "I knew you'd come around!" I cried, leaping into our humble two-seater skiff and unknotting the rope in a supersonic leap.

Pops' favorite hunting stop was Elkdead Island, and on a good day, he'd return back to the cabin with a hunk of deer meat and some camouflage paint smudged over his nose that Mama would fuss over for the entirety of the dinner meal until he washed up. It wouldn't take much too long to find him in the shallow sawgrass. The island didn't offer much in the way of tree cover, naturally making the job of gator hunting much cleaner than on the other side of the river.

I was out onto the river with a good shove of the arms and started on my way. Oars in, oars out. Oars in, oars out. And hope none of the gators are about.

About the Stone Soup Writing Workshop

The Stone Soup Writing Workshop began in March 2020 during the COVID-19-related school closures. In every session, a *Stone Soup* team member gives a short presentation, and then we all spend half an hour writing something inspired by the week's topic or theme. We leave our sound on so we feel as though we are in a virtual café, writing together in companionable semi-silence! Then, participants are invited to read their work to the group and afterward submit what they wrote to a special writing workshop submissions category. Those submissions are published as part of the workshop report on our blog every week. You can read more workshop pieces, and find information on how to register and join the workshop, at https://stonesoup.com/stone-soup-writing-workshop.

Honor Roll

Welcome to the Stone Soup Honor Roll. Every month, we receive submissions from hundreds of kids from around the world. Unfortunately, we don't have space to publish all the great work we receive. We want to commend some of these talented writers and artists and encourage them to keep creating.

STORIES

Nora Ahearn, 8
Anthony Caprara, 12
Ritam Chakrabarti, 13
Revaya Davis, 10
Colton Etheridge, 11
Olivia Hush, 11
Claudia Laurine, 8
Audrey Li, 12
Mohan Bharghav Rangavajjula, 8

PERSONAL NARRATIVES

Stella Langille, 9
Natalie Tang, 10
Erin Williams, 11

POETRY

Isha Patel Ahya, 11
Antoinette Katsas, 10
Iris Kindseth, 9
Dhilan Sethupathy, 9
Ismini Vasiloglou, 11

ART

Isolde Knowles, 9
Tang Li, 8

Books and magazines in the Stone Soup Store

Stone Soup makes a great gift!

Look for our books and magazines in our online store, Stonesoupstore.com, or find them at Amazon and other booksellers. If you use Amazon, be sure to add us as your Amazon Smile charity.

Published on September 1, 2020, *Three Days till EOC* by Abhimanyu Sukhdial, the winning novella in our 2019 Book Contest. Hardback, 72 pages, $9.99.

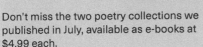

Don't miss the two poetry collections we published in July, available as e-books at $4.99 each.

Current and back issues available, older issues at reduced prices!

CPSIA information can be obtained
at www.ICGtesting.com
Printed in the USA
JSHW030227110521
14585JS00001B/2